COLIN MCCOOL SAVES CHRISTMAS

A DRUIDVERSE URBAN FANTASY NOVELETTE

M.D. MASSEY

"Click, c'mon—I thought you said you had this."
I was standing next to the quasi-god and trickster, shivering and huddling against a biting wind. The fierce gale blew hard, sending stinging pellets of ice and wet snow against my back, quickly soaking me to the bone. We'd just arrived somewhere that definitely was not Central Texas via Click's time magic spell, having traveled from the Hellpocalypse to our own timeline.

Obviously, something had gone wrong during the trip. That much was clear from the concerned look on the magician's face and the fact we'd ended up in a clime far removed from balmy Austin, Texas.

The magician's fine, boyish features scrunched up as he flashed me a sideways glance. "Tis' nuthin', lad—jest a miscalculation. I'll have us *there* in no time flat."

It was still unclear where "there" was, as the immortal magician formerly known as Gwydion had yet to say. He'd shown up in my druid grove in the other timeline a few hours prior, unannounced, and raving about my girlfriend being abducted. My first reaction to hearing the news was that Fallyn could take care of herself—she was an alpha werewolf, after all.

But Click had insisted we had to go rescue her. And after all that had happened over the last year, I wasn't about to take any chances where Fallyn's welfare was concerned. So, here we were.

Still, it'd be nice if One Flew Over the Cuckoo's Nest here would fill me in on where we're going.

Click pursed his lips as he fiddled with the luminescent glyphs and symbols floating between his hands in the air. "Didja' say sumthin', lad?"

"Nothing, just that I wish you'd hurry."

"Can't rush these things, ya' know. Terribly fickle, time magic is."

"Speaking of, what's with the visible magic? You've never done that before."

He answered without taking his eyes off his work. "Fer' troubleshooting a time magic spell, visual cues help. Now, instead o' standin' there gawkin', mayhaps ya' could do somethin' 'bout this cold."

"I'm a druid, not a weather wizard. But I'll see what I can do."

I rubbed my hands together, using the physical act as a focus for heating the surrounding air. The wind made it difficult to control, but I was able to bring the temperature up to a bearable fifty degrees or so. Although it was well above freezing, I was still damned uncomfortable, dressed as I was in summer fatigues, a t-shirt, and little else besides my Craneskin Bag and weaponry.

Should've scrounged up some warmer clothes before we left the other timeline. Live and learn.

Prior to our departure, Click mentioned that we'd be returning to our own timeline six months after I'd left—so, December-ish. He explained it away, saying something about critical convergences and inescapable time loops. That was stuff that went straight over my head, even though I'd learned enough time magic to travel between timelines. Central Texas rarely saw harsh winter weather, even in the dead of winter, so I figured I'd be okay in light pants and a t-shirt. Big mistake.

"Can you hurry it up? That's the best I can do in this wind without risking self-immolation, and I'm still freezing here. Speaking of which, where in the heck are we?"

"No idea, but not ta' worry, we'll be gone soon..." As his voice trailed off, the blood drained from Click's face. "Oh no."

I stamped my feet as I dug through my Bag,

searching for something warm to put on. "What now? Do I need to call us a ride-share?"

Click practically slapped my Bag out of my hands as he grabbed me by the front of my shirt. "Ya' don't understand, lad. We're not in the primary timeline. Somethin' interfered wit' the spell, an' we're someplace I ne'er intended ta' go, not in a million years."

I met his gaze, gauging the severity of the situation by parsing multiple clues. His pale complexion, the look of terror in his eyes, the way his hands blanched as they maintained a death grip on my t-shirt, and the fact that he hadn't already course-corrected and sent us on our merry way back home.

"That bad?" I asked, raising an eyebrow.

"Worse. The interference is still there, and I can't get ma' time magic ta' connect ta' our original timeline."

"Meaning, we're stranded?" He nodded in response like a dashboard bobblehead. As gently as possible, I peeled the magician's hands from my shirt. It was my last tee, after all, and I really didn't want him ripping it if we were lost. "Where exactly are we, Click?"

Ignoring my question, he looked around frantically. "Oh no, he's here. Whate'er ya' do, lad, don't tell him ya' joined the Trickster Local."

"Tell who?" I said, drawing Dyrnwyn and reaching out to connect with my Oak. If possible, I wanted to get us out of here—especially considering how terrified Click was presently. The magician was practically a god.

Anything that had him this frightened would be terrible, indeed.

Nothing. Either the Oak was in another dimension, or I hadn't bonded with it in this timeline. Just in case, I tried harder. *Shit, I can't even sense an Oak here.*

"Son of a... damn it, Click—where the hell did you take us?"

Click backed away, his face contorted in abject terror as he began preparing spells. Not only could I sense him gathering his magic, I could see it in the glow around his hands. The tricky little fucker was loading up for bear, from the look of it.

What has gotten into him?

"No time ta' explain. Run, lad!"

"Click—"

Fear had obviously sent him into one of his fits of madness, because he was clearly no longer in a rational state. Dyrnwyn hadn't lit up, however, so I knew that whatever was coming wasn't evil. As Click backed into the winter storm, iridescent magic swirling around him in a sphere that neither wind nor ice could penetrate, his eyes darted left and right, up and down. Obviously, whoever had interfered had blocked all his travel magic, else the magician would've been long gone.

"Well, hell," I muttered. *Best get ready to rumble.*

Glancing around nervously, I stealth-shifted and queued up a couple of spells. A fireball, some lightning, and—just in case—I held a stasis shield at about nine-tenths completion. The bummer was, I had to drop my heater cantrip to do it.

Freezing my ass off, again. I oughta' let him fight alone.

But, I wouldn't. If things went south, my plan was to cast the stasis shield around us both. Releasing it would completely drain my innate magic reserves, but if this thing was as bad as Click's hysteria indicated, I'd need a Hail Mary to save us. I only hoped that whatever was out there wasn't a god, because they *hated* humans who could use time magic. The last thing I needed was to be marked for death before we got out of this timeline.

One thing's for certain—I can always count on Click to drop me in the middle of a clusterfuck.

No sooner had I prepared for whatever might be coming, than a jovial baritone voice echoed from the dark.

"There you are, trickster. Didn't I tell you what would happen if you ever set foot in my world again?"

"'Twas an accident, I swear," Click said as he backed further into the storm. "We were jest passin' through, honest."

"Nevertheless, you were warned," the voice boomed.

"Click!" I yelled. "What should I do?"

"Nuthin', lad," he replied as he continued his retreat. "Jest' stay safe 'til I can come back fer' ya'!"

Within moments, he was far enough away to be completely obscured by the swirling snow and sleet. I slogged into the storm after him, spells at the ready, trying to home in on the sound of his voice.

"Yo, where are you?" I hollered as I leaned into the wind.

"No, you don't understand, lives are at stake!" Click's voice was a soft whine against the howling wind, barely loud enough for my Fomorian hearing to detect.

"That's always the case whenever you're involved, isn't it, magician?" the other voice replied. Strangely, I could hear him clear as a bell, despite the raging blizzard.

Further out in the dark, wintery night, there was a brilliant flash of light and energy. I was already squinting against the sleet and snow, so it didn't completely blind me, but it did take me by surprise. I slogged ahead, blinking the spots from my eyes even as the storm raged harder, creating white-out conditions.

Ahead, no more than ten feet away, I spotted a large, man-shaped silhouette. Too big to be Click, I knew it had to be the mysterious enemy that had him so thoroughly spooked.

Surprise, motherfucker.

I cut loose with both barrels, so to speak, releasing the fireball and the lightning bolt at once. The two spells coalesced in the air in front of my extended left palm, instantly shooting forth at my target with deadly precision. Fire and lightning lit up the night all around, orange on one side, cold blue on the other as they careened at the tall, broad, shadowy figure.

If the thing was as powerful as I thought, even the combined magic wouldn't kill it. But catching two elemental spells in the back was no picnic, either. I leapt after my spells, Dyrnwyn raised, planning to cleave the entity in two just after my magic staggered it.

2

Then, time slowed. I knew it was slowing because I could cast time magic, and hell if I didn't recognize chronourgy when I saw it. First, the lightning bolt and fireball both decelerated to a crawl, inching their way toward the intended target like two blazing, crackling snails. Next, just after reaching the apex of my leap, my forward momentum lagged as though I was moving through water.

Finally, both me and my spells stopped completely, but not before the spells got close enough to illuminate the stranger's tall, bulky figure. Frozen in midair, it was all I could do to watch as he spun halfway around at faster than full speed, almost vampire-fast, glancing over his shoulder to meet my gaze with piercing blue eyes.

I took stock of his appearance from head to toe

instantly, and realization hit me like the lightning bolt that hovered in midair between us. The black battered combat boots, the blood-red fatigues tucked into them, the leather coat dyed to match and trimmed in silvery-gray fur—not to mention his bushy white beard and mustache, as well as the pale gray hair that stuck out in tufts from under his fur-lined hood. I knew exactly who I faced.

Despite being caught in the weird, progressive stasis spell, I could still speak, and my astonished words flew out of my mouth before I knew what I was saying.

"Santy' Claus?"

His eyes widened slightly, and he turned fully around to address me. "Some call me that, yes, but they're mostly under the age of six. You can call me Claus. And I know you as well, Colin McCool, née Cailean mac Cumhaill, a.k.a. 'The Junkyard Druid,' last of Fionn's line."

"Wha'—I don't understand. You're real?"

His eyes narrowed as his gaze hardened, and for an instant, it felt as though he looked into my soul. Then, the sensation passed and his expression softened. "Ah, that explains it. Not where you come from, no. But here? Here I am as real as the snow melting on your skin."

Of course, this all makes sense. Time magic—of course he knows time magic. And Click? Hmm, leave it to him to cross Ol' Saint Nick.

"Wow, this is weird. And awkward. I mean, I just

jumped Santa. Shit." He glowered at me, and I demurred. "Sorry! It's just that I curse a lot when I'm stressed."

"Don't I know it," the jolly, not-so-fat man muttered.

"Since you know me, you also know this was all one big misunderstanding. Mind letting me down?"

He inclined his head, lowering his gaze to each of my spells in turn. "Mind banishing the elemental attacks, first?"

"Er, right."

With a mental command, the spells fizzled into sparks and ash, leaving us in darkness again. Suddenly, I found myself sailing through the air again, but when I landed, Santa was nowhere to be seen.

Odd, that—calling someone that name. As in, a real person. I glanced around, turning this way and that. *Nothing. Maybe I imagined it.*

I heard bells ringing behind me and spun around to look. There he was again, leading the biggest damned deer I'd ever seen through the snowstorm toward me. The deer was horse-sized, not quite a Clydesdale, but war horse tall for sure, and it was decked out in tack, like a riding horse minus the saddle. Small bells jangled on the sides of the hackamore that ran around its nose.

"Bells make it easier to find them in the driving snow," the big man proffered. "But they can be as silent if need be—that's why you didn't hear Donner before."

"Right. That's Donner. Er, gotcha."

"What did you expect, Rudolph?" he guffawed, slapping me on the shoulder.

"Um, yeah," I said, trying to stay calm while my brain struggled to make sense of everything. Finally, it latched onto a single, fairly important thought. "Say, you wouldn't happen to know where the guy I was with went, do you?"

Santa's expression soured instantly. "Oh, him. I sent him, well, elsewhere. He'll find his way home, eventually."

"Eh, not that I object—he's caused me more than a little grief over the years. But he was kind of my ride home." I looked around, trying to get my bearings in the surrounding blizzard. "Speaking of, where the heck am I?"

"Northern Canada, above the arctic circle," the big guy replied as he busied himself with checking Donner's tack. He tightened straps here and there as he rubbed and patted the animal down, barely glancing at me as he spoke. "As for your ride, that is unfortunate. Thankfully, your counterpart in this branch of the Twisted Paths has taken up permanent residence in Mag Mell. There, he wages continual war on the aes sídhe and Tuatha Dé Danann. So, there's no risk of you two meeting and causing the timeline to go on the fritz."

"Hmm, right." I chewed my lip. "That would be all well and good, except that Click—"

"That's what he's calling himself now? Wonder where he got that silly name."

"Er, no telling. Anyway, he's the one who cast the time magic spell that was supposed to take us from another timeline back to our own."

Kris Kringle nodded matter-of-factly. "And now you don't know how to return there—at least, not without Gwydion's assistance."

"Right."

He continued fussing over his giant reindeer, and I waited in silence for several seconds. It wasn't quite as cold in my half-Fomorian form, but I wasn't exactly comfortable, either. With nothing better to do, I cast the same heating cantrip I'd used earlier.

"Not as adept at druidry as the one from this time-line, I see," Ol' Saint Nick observed drily, speaking as if he were addressing his oversized ruminant. "But not as jaded, either. Somehow held on to the hope he knew in his youth, despite all the hardship and heartbreak. What do think, Donner? Should we offer him a deal?"

"A deal? You're a saint, for f—I mean goodness' sake. Aren't you supposed to help me out of the kindness of your heart?"

Santa pointed an index finger to the sky as he continued to fidget with the deer's tack. "Ah, but a saint of what? Certainly not of druids, I can tell you that."

Donner snorted and nudged the old but certainly

formidable man—or whatever he was—then the reindeer fixed me with a soft-eyed look.

"Hmm. Donner seems to like you, although I shan't be surprised, what with your affinity for animals. Still, he's an excellent judge of character, so I suppose we can give it a shot."

"Thank you, Donner," I said, addressing the reindeer directly and meaning it. Donner lowered his head slightly, scratching the ground with a forehoof. I turned my gaze back to the old saint. "But give what a shot?"

"A deal, a task assigned, one good turn for another." He must've seen something in my expression, as next he smiled and waved dismissively. "Oh, nothing like those foul, fallen fae might offer. I am a saint, after all, and not given to acts of treachery and deception. This will be a fair deal, true as the North Star, I can assure you of that. Besides, I seem to be a bit shorthanded of late, as this year those blighted offspring of Hel decided to act in tandem, if not in concert, for once."

"Wait, you mean the Krampuses—Krampusi? I thought they were your helpers, or something."

"For one, there's only one Krampus, and you should hope you never run into him. Second, what makes you think a saint would ever accept the help of one of Loki's descendants, much less ally with them?"

"Um, half-titan here," I said, raising my hand sheepishly. "Sort of the same thing, isn't it?"

He cast me a kind, almost fatherly look before

addressing the deer again. "Sells himself short, like the druid master we know as well. Too bad that one started believing his own lies. Shame."

"Am I some sort of—I don't know—*villain* in this timeline?"

Santa Claus gave a short shake of his head. "Best to avoid asking questions that you don't want answered, yes? Now, about that task I need taken care of..."

I rubbed a hand across my face before fixing the broad-shouldered saint with a stern gaze. "You swear you'll do right by me? Meaning, I do this for you, and you'll send me to my own timeline, and not five-hundred years in the future, or ten-thousand years in the past, but where Click and I were headed before we ended up here?"

"I don't swear—at all—but yes, I will do right by you. A promise like that one is binding, especially to a saint."

"Alright," I sighed. "Tell me what you need me to do."

"Excellent," he boomed. "Now, then—ever hear of a town called Fredericksburg?"

3

The job was simple, according to Claus. We'd taken shelter under a rocky overhang, hidden by a copse of trees. I had a fire going, and the man in red was explaining the job to me.

"Some of Krampus' underlings are trying to ruin Christmas in Fredericksburg. Your job is to make sure they do not."

I rubbed my chin, brow furrowed. "Forgive me for being skeptical, but it seems a little too simple to me." Claus gazed at me beatifically, looking for all the world as if he were free from guile or malice. When he failed to provide comment, I continued. "When you say 'ruining Christmas,' what exactly do you mean by that?"

"Ah, there's a question I can answer. Generally speaking, these creatures operate by stealing the Christmas spirit from people. How they do it varies, but it usually involves inciting arguments, misplacing presents, hacking bank accounts, and other, more nefarious crimes. Whatever they can do to get a human's mind off giving and helping others and onto fear, sadness, envy, greed, and resentment, that's their goal."

"That's it?" I asked, trying not to show too much incredulity.

His eyes rolled upward for a moment as he pursed his lips—or I think he did, as his bushy beard and mustache covered his mouth. "There is one other thing," he replied, tapping a finger to his lips before pointing it at me. "They have a tendency to steal children. Never more than one at a time, as it draws too much attention. But they will snatch a child if given the opportunity."

"That's a familiar tune," I hissed through gritted teeth. "So, what are the rules of engagement?"

He chuckled and clutched his tummy, which looked pretty damn flat under all that leather and fur. "You mean to ask, can you kill them? Most certainly, as they'll kill you in a heartbeat."

Rubbing my hands together, I gave the man in red a grim smile. "Finally, some good news."

Claus clapped his hands on his thighs. "Well, then, it's settled. I'll summon the rest of the team, and we'll drop you off in Fredericksburg, just in time for their annual Christmas parade. Those miscreants are sure to show up there, eager to spoil the fun."

"Um, hang on a second. I might want some back up

for this one. Drop me off in Austin, and I'll make my way to F-burg from there."

Claus swung his head round, frowning. "You mean to recruit help from your former associates? I doubt that's a good idea."

"When you say 'former,' you mean, 'no longer associated'—not dead, right?"

The big man waved his hands back and forth. "I've already said too much. Suffice it to say that your counterpart in this timeline has not maintained cordial relations with many of the people you know and trust."

"Meh, they're still the same people, right? Once I explain what I'm doing, they'll come around. Just drop me off at Luther's, and I'll handle things from there."

Claus lowered his chin as he cocked his head, looking at me from beneath a hooded brow. "Are you sure you want to do this?"

"Positive."

He harrumphed softly. "Fine. But don't say I didn't warn you." He pulled off one of his black leather gloves, sticking two fingers in his mouth to release a sharp, high whistle. Then, he gave me a reassuring nod. "They should be here shortly."

Moments later, I heard sleigh bells in the distance, even over the storm. "Wait a minute—you mean I get to ride in the sled?"

Claus frowned. "It's a sleigh, not a sled. And it's not as exciting as it sounds."

"Whatever. This is turning out to be the best free-lance gig ever."

I quickly extinguished the fire, eager to get my ride with Santy Claus. As we exited the copse, the "sleigh" pulled into view, materializing out of the driving snow and sleet like a phantom ship emerging from a dense fog. It would've been creepy, if not for living, breathing reindeer pulling the thing.

Speaking of, seven of them were hitched to the sleigh, with space for Donner at the front right position. The others were more or less carbon copies of the first, and the sleigh looked like something off a Christmas card. That was to say, if you ignored the 20 mm cannons fore and aft, and the forward-facing batteries of air-to-air and air-to-surface missiles mounted to the rails starboard and port. I chose to overlook the weaponry, hopping over the side onto the plush velvet rear seat of the shiny brass and red-lacquered vehicle.

"This is like a dream come true," I said, giddy with excitement.

Claus answered as he hitched Donner to the sleigh. "Ah, about that—"

"A real flight in Santa's sleigh," I continued, ignoring the saint completely. "Wait until I tell Hemi."

Claus shook his head, then he mounted up in the front seat with a grimace plastered across his face. He snapped the reins, and the deer started forward, pulling the sleigh with ease. Then, a 12-foot-wide magic portal opened in front of the team, and we slid through—right into the back parking lot behind Luther's café.

"What, no flight? Seriously?"

Claus turned, flashing me a sheepish grin as he shrugged. "Oh, they can take to the air, but I stopped flying a long time ago. My reindeer have the unlimited power to portal me anywhere on Earth, and doing so keeps me from having to use the ordinance. Can't tell you how many times the PLA have tried to shoot us down, never mind the Taliban with their shoulder-fired anti-aircraft missiles and every loon with a deer rifle taking pot shots at us. Sorry to disappoint, but this is how I travel now."

"Man, this job sucks," I groused as I leapt out of the sleigh. Claus gave me a look that said I was treading on thin ice, so I made a placating gesture with my hands. "My apologies for being rude. It's just that I always wanted to fly on your sleigh. Anyway, I appreciate the ride, and I'll see you when the job's done."

"Oh no, I'm not leaving," he said, hopping lightly to the ground. "I've decided to stick around for this."

"Okay, but... um... won't your presence here, I dunno —draw attention?"

"I'm Santa, kid. They can't see me unless I want them to."

"Ah, right. I keep trying to get Click to show me how to do that, but he won't budge." Since Claus didn't offer to dish either, I turned to look at the café, which was decidedly dark and boarded up. There were lights on upstairs, though. "Huh, I guess Luther moved shop in this timeline or something. Did he rent the apartment out to another vamp?"

The jolly man's face was poker player neutral as he replied. "Oh, he's up there, alright. Perhaps you should knock? Although he already knows someone is out here."

"Right, vampire hearing. Give me a sec', eh?"

Claus gave a one-armed 'after you' gesture, stepping aside as I strolled to the back door of the shop. I knocked three times, no answer, so I stepped back a few feet and tossed a pebble at the upstairs window.

"Yo, Luther—it's me, Colin. Open up."

Luther's face appeared in the window upstairs, glaring down with a look of incredulity. Then he disappeared, and the back door opened. Luther stood there in white silk pajamas, a matching white silk robe trimmed in white fur, and white fluffy slippers. He had a bloody Cosmopolitan in one hand and a cigarette smoldering at the end of a quellazaire in the other.

Leaning against the doorframe, he sneered only slightly as looked me up and down. "So, Colin McCool darkens my door. To what do I owe the pleasure?"

"Hey, Luther, sorry to bother you this late, but I need help." The vampire chuckled mirthlessly in reply, rolling his eyes as he looked up and away to puff on the quellazaire. "What's so funny?"

"What indeed, druid," he drawled in his low yet slightly feminine voice. "Don't you remember the last time you asked for my help? Why in the hell would I fall for that doe-eyed song and dance shit a second time, hmm?"

"Er, I sort of remember, but refresh my memory."

Claus snorted softly behind me. "Oh, this will be good."

Luther sipped his drink, then he took a long, dramatic puff from his cigarette, exhaling through his nostrils before pointing it at me. "Since you seem to have suffered a temporary loss of memory, allow me to assist. You used me to get to a high fae delegation that was visiting the local court from overseas. The assassination of those delegates nearly caused an all-out war between the Vampyri and the Fae. Of course, you high-tailed it back to your fortress, long before the rest of us suffered the consequences. So, no—whatever it is you want, you can fuck right off to wherever you came from."

"Luther, I—"

He tossed the remnants of his drink at my feet, cutting me off. "Save it, and piss off. While you do that, Ima march my happy ass back upstairs to watch a Hallmark movie and root for the token lesbian couple." He spun on heel, glancing over his shoulder for a parting shot. "Have a nice life, Colin—whatever's left of it."

The door slammed in my face, although I never saw

Luther place a hand on it. I stood there dumbfounded until Claus cleared his throat. "Perhaps we should move on to the next person you'd like to see?"

"Of course, of course. Let's swing by the junkyard."

Claus merely nodded silently, mounting up after me. When we arrived at the address seconds later, the junkyard was gone, replaced by high-rise condominiums. Yet, I knew we were at the right address—it was plastered on the brass plaque by the front door, after all.

"Yo, what happened to my junkyard?" I said, standing up in the sleigh.

"Your counterpart sold it years ago," Claus replied. "I believe his justification was 'too many bad memories' or something."

"Crap," I said, eliciting a wince from the jolly man. "Sorry, habit. What happened to Finnegas and Maureen?"

Claus *tsked* as he tilted his head. "Finnegas passed on due to an overdose. Your counterpart found him in a van, cold and lifeless one morning. Maureen ran Eire Imports until the day of his passing, then she sold all the Seer's earthly possessions and placed the money into a trust in your counterpart's name, at his instruction. Since then, she's been seen from time to time, mostly collecting bounties for the various factions."

"Seriously? Not only did I sell the junkyard, but I fired Maureen?"

"In a manner of speaking, yes."

Plopping back down on the plush velvet seat, I exhaled heavily. "Let's go to Hemi's place."

A moment later, we passed through a portal, exiting on the street in front of Hemi's garage apartment. "Well, that's good news. Some things never change, I guess."

Claus said nothing, so I disembarked the sleigh, strolling down the drive toward Hemi's place with a bit more pep in my step. I knocked "shave and a haircut, two bits" on his door and waited for him to open it. When no one did, I knocked again, harder this time. Soon I heard someone cursing in a decidedly Kiwi accent, followed by the rattling of empty cans and heavy, plodding footsteps.

The door opened, and the first thing I noticed was Hemi in stained red and gray plaid boxers, an equally stained and tattered forest green terrycloth bathrobe, and nothing else. He lacked his tā moko, although it looked as though the rest of his ink was intact. Yet, he also sported a three-day beard, bags under his eyes, and hair that had grown into ratty, matted dreads. His face looked bloated, his belly as well, and his skin was ashen and sallow.

He took one look at me, *hmphed*, and punched me in the face, hard. Then he slammed the door as I fell flat on my back. Shaking it off, I noticed a pair of black boots standing beside me.

"That went well," Claus said without a hint of sarcasm.

"How so?" I mumbled, rubbing my jaw as I slowly pushed myself off the concrete drive.

"The last time he saw you, he tried to kill you. From what I gather, you were forced to portal away to avoid someone's death, whether his or your own. Since then, the threat of mutually assured destruction has kept you away from his presence."

I set my jaw back into place with a pop, working it around in circles to ensure it still functioned properly. "I assume further such visits to my other friends and acquaintances will go just as smashingly?"

"You assume correct. Fallyn is in charge of the Austin Pack now. Her father died in a ruckus that resulted from your counterpart's assassination of the Vampire coven leader who took over after the Council removed Luther. After that catastrophe, she put out a bounty on your head. Needless to say, you no longer have Pack privileges."

"Ah. And Belladonna? Crowley?"

"Belladonna returned to Spain after your counterpart broke her heart for the third time. She has also sworn to kill you on sight. Crowley remains here in Austin, performing dark rites in his tower aerie and doing his adoptive mother's will."

"What? He's still working for Fuamnach?"

"Indeed," Claus replied with a curt nod. "Shall I go on?"

I pressed my palms into my forehead. This was all

giving me a massive headache. "No, that's quite enough. But what went wrong?"

Claus gave a grim shake of his head. "Your counterpart lost faith, Colin. Circumstances caused him to harden his heart, to become callous, cruel, and pessimistic. He chose vengeance over valor, selfishness over charity, solitude over companionship. Without your positive, encouraging influence and heroic example, all these people's lives were so much worse for the lack thereof."

"Well, sh..." I paused. "I mean, shoot. That's just not cool."

"No, it's not cool at all. And it looks like you're doing this job solo."

"That's alright, I could use the workout. Can I impose on you for one last ride to Fredericksburg?"

"It would be my pleasure," the jolly man said. Before heading for the sleigh, he flashed me a sympathetic smile. "And, Colin?"

I was somewhat lost in thought, although I'd been looking right at him. "Whah? I mean, what do you need, Claus?"

"When you get back to where you came from, keep the faith. One bright spark of hope can make a world of difference."

Claus marched off before I could answer, leaving me with plenty to think about.

4

Claus dropped me off in a secluded area of Baron's Creek, not far from downtown yet away from prying eyes. As I climbed out of the sleigh, he cleared his throat to get my attention. "Do not underestimate the servants of Krampus. All of them are either the offspring of minor gods or former humans so twisted by magic that they possess similar powers."

"How many should I expect to run into?"

He hitched a shoulder in a half-shrug. "A half-dozen? More? It can vary, but assume you'll be badly outnumbered. I do have a man in the area, but I'm uncertain if he'll be able to assist, so you're mostly on your own."

"Great. Anything else I should know?"

"The straw ones burn pretty easily, but the fur-covered ones are tougher than nails. They're basically demons, so anything blessed slows them down."

"Huh."

"Huh, what?"

I scrunched my face up. "I wasn't sure if any of that was real. I mean, it doesn't work on vampires."

Claus clucked his tongue. "Vampires are merely altered humans. They have a soul. However, the soulless are quite susceptible." He grabbed the reins, and another large portal appeared ahead of his team. "Watch your back. I'll know as soon as the mission is successful, at which point I'll fulfill my end of the bargain."

"Not going to wish me good luck?"

"We saints don't believe in luck, Colin. You really need to spend more time at mass." He snapped the reins, and the sleigh headed through the portal. "And go to confession," he said as the portal began to wink out behind him. "It'll do you good."

"Thanks for the guilt!" I hollered after him, but the portal had already closed. "Confession? No thanks, I'm messed up enough as it is," I muttered, glancing around to get my bearings. "Blessed weapons, huh? Wonder where I can get a set of +5 blessed plate armor around here. Eh, I'll just have to settle for holy water, I guess."

There was a Catholic church just up the hill, one of those old-school creepy ones with the not-quite lifelike statues of the saints that always seemed to be staring at you, no matter where you stood in the church. I'd visited there on a high school trip once, and I knew they had a stoup up front. Whistling *Jingle Bells*, I headed up the creek bank in that general direction.

As it happened, I passed in front of the restaurant and warehouse where I'd first met Nameless the night raven. *More like first fought. Damned thing shat all over my seats as I recall. Had a hell of a time getting the smell out.*

I marched on by, resisting the urge to stop in and feast on pizza and pie. I was nearly past the place and on my way to Main Street when I saw a flash of gray fur darting into the alley behind a shop up the street. Normally I'd have written it off as a stray dog or cat, but something wasn't right with the scene in front of the store. A family stood there, the parents arguing while their two kids—a girl aged around nine and a boy of about six—looked on.

"I didn't have the keys, Daryl—you did," the woman said with exasperation and barely contained contempt in her voice.

"And I told you, I stuck them in your purse when we were at the restaurant," the man snapped.

"Well, they're not there. Go back and ask at the restaurant again. Maybe someone turned them in."

The man shook his head. "I already did that, Marlene. Asking again isn't going to make the keys magically appear."

The wife threw her hands up in the air. "So, how are

we going to get home? I don't think we can call a ride-share to take us all the way to Round Rock."

"I don't know," her hubby snapped. "I guess I'll have to call a locksmith."

"We can't afford a locksmith, Daryl, not this close to Christmas."

I saw where this was going, and I also noticed that the boy was looking around the corner, where I'd seen that flash of fur moments before. Instead of paying attention to the parents, I cued in on the convo he was having with his sister.

"But I saw it, Allison—honest!"

"You're such a liar, Jackson. There's no such thing as a goat man."

"Yeah-huh there is, and he took Mom's keys. Then, he ran around the back of the building."

Bingo.

While the family members were all distracted, I cast a chameleon spell on myself and headed after the "goat man." Since I was still in my stealth-shifted form—half-human, half-Fomorian—I wasn't too concerned about a fight with a single goat-demon thingie. Still, it never hurt to be careful. Since I hadn't retrieved any holy water yet, I readied a spell.

Demons were notoriously resistant to elemental magic, so I opted for something that was more defensive in nature. Namely, a quicksand spell that would turn the earth into a slurry, then rapidly change it solid again. Unless the thing could phase—and I doubted it could— once trapped, I'd be able to question it safely and at will.

That was the plan, at least. However, when I traipsed around the back corner of the building, I found not one goat man, but six. Even worse, they clearly saw right through my chameleon spell.

"Baah, look at this chuhhhhmp," one of them bleated. "That dime store magic isn't going to hide you from us, hedge wizard. Illusions are our specialty."

Like the rest, he was all goat from the waist down and humanoid from the waist up, save for his bizarre, half-human and half-goat face and head. The only way to describe it would be to imagine if a goat was morphing into a human, and got stuck halfway between. That's what its face looked like, complete with two longish, curving horns sticking out of its forehead.

The body was covered in short, salt and pepper fur, from its cloven feet, up its weird, backward-looking legs, to the tips of its elongated, pointed ears. Its eyes were yellow, with vertically slitted pupils similar to most predators, versus the horizontal pupils real goats had. Instead of the elongated nose I'd expected from one of Krampus' offspring, it had two slits and an upper mandible that sloped down to a protruding lower jaw. It snarled at me, revealing a mouthful of pointed, razor-sharp teeth.

No grass grazers here, that's for sure.

By the time I'd sized the first one up, the others turned to gaze at me, braying at me with this peculiar, honking, repetitive bark. The cacophony was overwhelming, and while I wasn't quite certain what it meant, I was pretty sure they were pissed. As they spread out to flank me, I raised my hands in a warding gesture.

"Hang on there, fellas. No need for this to get ugly. As a courtesy, I'm going to give you the chance to leave town of your own volition."

Rather than respond verbally, the lot of them increased the bizarre goat noises they'd been making, adding in a bit of teeth-gnashing and spittle flecking for good measure.

"I'll take that as a 'no.' Fine, have it your way."

I cut loose with my spell, aiming it at the center of the group. Although I had the spell on "instacast," no spell is instantaneous. All magic requires at least a split-second to produce the intended effect. My quicksand spell was no different, and apparently this wasn't the goat dudes' first rodeo. No sooner had I pointed at the ground and released the spell, than all six of them leapt in different directions.

Two of them jumped on top of the building, an impressive feat by any standard. Two more jumped atop a chain link fence nearby, balancing on the top rail like some sort of oddball circus act. And the other two leapt at the wall of the building, turning in midair to land hooves first, at which point they ran at me sideways, defying gravity and all sorts of other laws of physics.

Well, hell. Guess I should've stopped by the church first.

5

The immediate threat were the two goat demons coming at me along the wall. Rather than engage in hand-to-hand with them—never a good idea when outnumbered—I instead cast my old faithful, get-out-of-jail-free, insta-cast spell. With only a thought, the flash-bang spell released in an explosion of light, sound, and pressure from my extended hand, directly in the face of the first goat man.

Granted, the effect was always greater at night and inside enclosed spaces, but the spell was still not pleasant at close range. The goat man who got it full in the snout brayed and faltered mid-step, stumbling to the ground at my feet as I backed away. However, his compadre wasted no time worrying about his partner's state of wellbeing, stepping on the fallen goat man's back and leaping right at me.

Meanwhile, the two goats on the fence and the two on the roof were advancing and angling for a pincer attack. *Screw it, time to dance.*

Reaching back with my left hand, I pushed Dyrnwyn's sheath up and slightly over my right shoulder, grasping it near the end. Grabbing the hilt with my dominant hand, I drew the sword over my shoulder while pulling down on the sheath. A breakaway sheath would've been better, but I was working with what I had, and my practiced draw was quick enough to beat the attack. Dyrnwyn's satin gray blade flared along its length with a brilliant, blue-white light as I brought it down directly on the advancing goat man's shoulder, cleaving the thing in two from collar to groin.

Blood splattered my face and torso as the body fell like flower petals to either side of me. I glared at the other goat demons through the nearly blinding flames that ran up and down Dyrnwyn's length. The lot of them paused almost in unison, unsure of what they should do.

I reversed my grip on the sword's hilt, stabbing it downward through the breastbone of the downed, blinded goat man. Seeing yet another of their number die so easily must've made up their minds for them. The remaining four turned tail and headed away from me, two of them leaping from rooftop to rooftop, the other two landing lightly on the other side of the fence and sprinting in the direction of the creek.

Shit. I was hoping they'd fight and make this easy.

Besides, these things were fast. I made a hasty, spur of the moment choice—more like a mental flip of a coin, really—and headed after the goat men above me. With two running strides, I leapt off the ground with a grunt, landing on the tarred roof of the nearest building with little effort.

Thank goodness for Fomorian strength.

I was as strong as most young vampires and some werewolves in this form, and nearly as fast, so reaching the rooftop at a run was hardly a challenge. That said, these goat man whatzits could move, and I found myself losing ground on them before we'd gone two blocks.

Fortunately, the downtown Main Street area of Fredericksburg was only about six blocks by four blocks, so the goat creatures would run out of ground soon. Once they took to the streets, they'd have to navigate cars, people, and animals—everyone brought their dogs with them in the Texas Hill Country—and being glamoured and functionally invisible would provide little advantage in that regard.

Vaulting HVAC units and hurdling vent pipes and fan turbines, I did my best to keep my quarry in sight as we neared the end of our elevated journey. With one more block to go, I expected them to leap across the next side street, as they'd done for the last three blocks. Instead, they surprised me, veering right and dropping off the backside of the building, the trailing goat man sparing me a single sideways glance and braying snort before it dropped out of sight.

Fearing I was about to lose track of my prey, I put on a burst of speed, skidding to a stop at the edge of the building where the goats had jumped off. No way was I going to leap off the side blind. At best, I might be jumping on a crowd of people, and at worst, straight into an ambush. Yet, no crowds or ambushes awaited me down there. Instead, all I saw were a few sawhorse-style construction barriers surrounding an open manhole in the alley below.

Sewers. I hate sewers.

With a sigh, I sheathed Dyrnwyn and leapt into the manhole. As soon as I cleared street level on my descent into darkness, I knew I'd made a mistake. Not because the goat men were waiting for me, but because the smell of human waste was overwhelming. I landed with a sort of gurgling splash in knee-deep sewage, nearly slipping as I bent my knees to absorb the force of the fall.

The tunnels were narrow, leaving little room to swing a longsword. It was a bad place to use elemental magic, too, what with the tight confines and risk of a methane explosion. That eliminated firearms as well, so I drew a long knife from a sheath that was mounted horizontally at the small of my back.

Man, I'll never get the smell out of these clothes. Maybe Claus will let me stop by Wally World before I head back home.

That was, if I completed the mission. Glancing up and down the tunnel while trying to ignore the wet, oozing sensation that was sewage seeping into my combat boots, I saw no sign of my quarry. Sensory enhancement to track them by smell was also out of the question, for obvious reasons, and I heard nothing but the sounds of water dripping and human waste flowing all around.

As for direction of pursuit, there were only two choices, but I didn't like fifty-fifty odds. If I guessed wrong, they'd be long gone before I reversed course. Instead, I decided to resort to good old druid magic.

Normally, I'd have to change my breathing patterns to drop into a druid trance, but recently, I'd had my full knowledge of druid mastery restored. Shortly after that, I'd spent considerable time in my druid grove under the tutelage of a god. Lugh didn't invent druidry, but he was a master of it, as was the case with everything he put his hand to. His instruction had allowed me to advance farther along the path.

It took no more than a thought to enter the trance and extend my senses outward. Seconds later, my consciousness connected with several of the rats that made this sewer tunnel their home. The question was, east or west?

My mind skittered across theirs, first following a trail of rat minds to the west. That soon proved to be a waste of time, so I switched direction. The rodents further down the east tunnel had heard something splashing in the muck moments before, and they'd also picked up an odd smell, one that was animal and foreign to the sewers.

Not only that, but they were hiding, their natural survival instincts telling them that predators were about. I gathered all this information instantly, disconnecting from their thoughts but keeping my senses open to connection. That would allow me to skate across the surface thoughts of rats that hid further along the tunnels. Those whose thoughts had been disturbed would lead me to the goat men—and, hopefully, their hideout.

They have to have some sort of leader. That's the way it always works with creatures like these. The betas follow the alpha.

None of the goat men I'd encountered above struck me as being particularly dominant, so I expected to find someone or something in charge at their rendezvous point. Hopefully, it wouldn't be Krampus. Based on what Claus had said, I assumed he—it?—was some sort of minor deity.

Claus took out Click without breaking a sweat. So, how powerful is his nemesis?

I honestly didn't care to find out. After this job was over, I had to return to my own timeline to rescue Fallyn from the entity that had spirited her away by use of time magic. Next on the agenda after that was a trip back to the Hellpocalypse to save that timeline's version of the shadow wizard Crowley from his evil foster mother, Fuamnach.

And after that? Then, I had a war to wage with the Vampyri, who now ruled the Hellpocalypse. Good times.

Better keep my mind on current matters. These things seem to be pretty tricky.

I'd traveled another block east underground, following the trail of freaked out rodents in a straight line. Up ahead, the sewer tunnel ended in an intersection of sorts, where the flow of sewage and rainwater drained into pipes along the floor of the junction. I entered the tunnel intersection on high alert, as the rats had scattered from this area, and there was nowhere else to go.

Something's not right with the wall up ahead. An illusion?

Figuring it might be how they escaped the sewers, I crossed the intersection and approached the wall. Just as I switched from my normal vision into the magical spectrum, the sewage erupted all around me. Four goat men leapt out of the filthy water, converging on me and pulling me down into the muck.

6

Two of them landed on my shoulders, pinning my arms to my sides as they dragged me down. The other two latched onto my legs, lifting and pulling me off my feet so I had no leverage to defend the tackle. Soon I was completely underwater and held down by all four goat men, who apparently meant to drown me.

Great, now I'm going to smell like goats and sewage. Peachy.

I'd been in tight spots like this before, each time surviving by luck, guile, or magic. Thing was, these goat men were strong, much stronger than I'd anticipated. I could hold my breath for a while in my half-Fomorian form, but eventually they'd figure out I wasn't dying and they'd start biting and clawing.

While my flesh and bone structure were mostly Fomorian and very tough, my skin wasn't, and they could easily rip it to shreds. I didn't fancy the idea of bleeding to death in a sewer, so I decided to act.

Physically, the four goat men were more than a match for me in this form. I could manage one or two of them—more, if I had room to swing a sword—but they'd gotten the jump on me and had me at a disadvantage. I could shift into my full Fomorian form, but it'd take precious seconds to complete the transformation, and they'd certainly rip me apart before I could complete it. That left one option only, one I was more than happy to exercise.

Magic it is, then.

Druidry wasn't the type of magic that you typically used in tense situations. That's because we druids worked with the flow and rhythms of nature, harnessing the earth's energies and amplifying or focusing them with magic. Mainstream magic was a lot more forceful and direct, because it warped nature's forces or drew energy from other dimensions to achieve the desired effect.

The bottom line was that most druid spells took time to prepare and use. We didn't like to disrupt the natural order—the butterfly effect, and all that. The last thing any druid wanted to do was draw too much energy too quickly and cause a natural disaster on the other side of the globe.

Minor cantrips that required little energy could be cast at will, but anything manipulating greater forces required more groundwork. For that reason, we typically prepared spells in advance, storing the necessary power until needed. Or we made sure we had time to prepare before a major casting. Johnny on the spot, a druid was not.

What I intended to do was to freeze the surface of the water by drawing heat out of it all at once. Hopefully, then I could squirm free while the goat men were busy extricating themselves and freezing their asses off. Hope made for poor planning in most cases, but I was three feet underwater in a sewer fighting four goat demon thingies, so I was working with what I had.

I started by connecting with the water at a molecular level, which took some doing because of all the filth floating around in it. Then I had to measure how much heat was present so I could know how much to remove. By the time I figured all that out, I realized that the goat men were dragging me toward the wall.

What the...?

I'd stopped struggling to play dead and focus on casting my spell, but now I was concerned that had been a tactical error. I sensed that we were passing through an illusion of some sort, likely whatever concealed the entrance to their lair. They pulled me through an opening in the wall, snagging my leg on the rough edge as they dragged me past.

No worries, I can still cast this spell and get free. Three... two... one...

With a thought, I flipped the switch on the flow of energy that would remove heat from above me and freeze the nasty sewage on the surface. However, nothing happened. I wasn't disconnected from my magic—it simply fizzled out when I released it.

Shit! They must've pulled me into an anti-magic field.

Even worse, the field was blocking my shifter abilities. Although on the surface I looked the same, beneath my skin I felt my bones losing density, my muscles losing strength. That's when I really started to panic, because I could hold my breath two to three minutes tops in my human form, and I'd already burned a ton of oxygen.

I tried using the knife in my hand to cut one of them, but the goat man holding me on that side simply knocked it out of my grasp. Kicking and wriggling was a waste of energy, because they each easily had the strength of five grown men. But fight I did, more out of desperation than anything, using up what little oxygen I had left, until my lungs were burning and I was nearly ready to inhale sewage into my lungs.

I thought I was done with near-drowning experiences after that jaunt in Underhill. Survive an attack by a water goddess, only to be drowned by a goat. Lame.

Just as I was about to either suck sewer water or pass out, the goat men hauled me above the surface. Each one held a limb, keeping me stretched out spread eagle-style, but that was okay because the will to fight had temporarily left me. All I could do was sputter filthy water and suck in dank, malodorous, blessed air.

After a few seconds I opened my eyes, and muck-covered as they were, the anti-magic glyphs on the ceiling stood out like a carrot on a snowman's face. They looked Norse or Germanic in origin, similar to Elder Futhark but more sinister in appearance. We were inside a naturally formed limestone cavern, which were quite common to the Texas Hill Country, this chamber being roughly twenty by forty feet.

The runes covered the ceiling and walls all around. I imagined they were intended to prevent the jolly man from scrying on the goat men. They'd also serve as protection against any local human magic-user who might attempt to drive them away.

The goat men began tying me up while I was still getting my bearings, hands bound behind my back and ankles together. Then they dragged me out of the filthy water, up a short embankment. There they dropped me unceremoniously on the hard limestone floor, next to an iron cage that looked like something that might hang outside the walls of a medieval castle.

What are those things called? A giblet? Gibbet? Yeah, that's it.

While I was examining the cage and wondering why they hadn't killed me, a shrill voice echoed across the cavern. "What in the name of Hel is that?"

I glanced across the cavern, scooting to a seated position with my back to the cage as I did so. There a seven-foot-tall goat man stooped as he entered, scraping his long, curving, spiraled horns as he passed under the arched limestone opening. He was similar in form to the goat men who had captured me, but rather than being made of flesh and fur, this goat man was made of straw.

Weird, the straw moves in bundles like muscle. Reminds me a bit of those feldgeisters we fought that served the Roggenmutter.

The other goat men all did a weird curtsey as the straw bockman—German for "goat man," because that's what these things were—entered the room.

"Some sort of demon huhhhn-ter, great Buttnmandl. He attacked us in the town above, so we am-baaaah..."

My coughing, hacking fit of laughter interrupted the goat man who had answered his master. One of the others closer to me kicked me in the ribs, which hurt like hell, but for the life of me I could not stop laughing.

"Why is the human laughing?" the shrill-voiced straw bockman asked his underling.

"I don't *bah* know, my liege. Shall I ask him?"

"Yes, fool! He might be planning an escape, or feigning weakness as some sort of ruse. For all we know, the Fat Man heads here as we speak."

That last sentence elicited a chorus of grumbles from the rest of the goat men, mostly consisting of curses aimed at Claus and threats against my life.

"Silence!" the straw goat man commanded. As the

chittering from his underlings died down, he pointed one long, clawed, straw finger at me. "Ask him."

"Dude, I'm sitting right here," I muttered, earning me another kick in the gut.

The goat who'd spoken up click-clacked over to me on his cloven feet, then he squatted and grabbed me by my jaw with his furry, clawed hand. "Speak, human. Tell us what you find so amusing. The great Buttnmandl demands it."

As he let go of my face, I sniggered, despite being covered in muck and having the shit kicked out of me. "That's why. That, right there."

The other goat men looked around the cavernous chamber, searching left and right, high and low. "You speak in riddles, *bah* human. Explain yourself."

I ignored the peckerwood in front of me, turning to address his boss instead. "You seriously mean to tell me your name is 'Butt Mandel'?" I said, busting out laughing. "Is that Yiddish for 'ass man' or something? Was there a mixup at the DMV?"

Butt Mandel was not amused, and his voice took on a sinister tone as he hissed instructions to his toadies. "Beat him, then lock him in the cage. We'll sacrifice him to Hel later."

7

Getting curb-stomped by goat boy and his buddies was not the highlight of my week. Turns out that cloven feet tend to cut skin when you catch the edge. Luckily, these clowns didn't seem to have much enthusiasm for the job, eager as they were to get topside before the big parade.

After five minutes of tap-dancing on my rib cage, they left me bruised and bleeding on a bed of moldy, matted straw inside the gibbet. Of course, they'd taken my Crane-skin Bag and all my gear from me, including Dyrnwyn. *Lousy pieces of shit.* The Bag would make it back to me eventually, but I couldn't afford to lose Dyrnwyn. Hopefully, they stashed it instead of dumping my stuff in the drink.

I'd like to say I waited until I was sure they were gone before trying to escape, but truthfully, I was in no mood to do anything following the beating I took. After about an hour spent alternating between wishing my Fomorian healing factor would mysteriously kick in and wishing I was dead, a squeaking noise near my cage brought me back to reality.

With a long, pitiful groan, I lifted my head and turned to see what was making all the racket. It probably wasn't that loud, but when you have a concussion, every noise is an assault. It took some time for me to spot him, but there was a rat sitting on his haunches outside the cage, twitching his whiskers and squeaking up a storm.

He was gray all over, and slightly mangy, with long, crooked whiskers, a wet pink nose, and beady, intelligent eyes. His tail seemed to be missing the tip, and it looked as though another rat had gnawed off part of his left ear as well. But, all things considered, I had to admit —he was charming, in a scraggly sort of way.

"Hey, little guy," I said through swollen lips as I struggled to push myself upright. "Where'd you come from? Oh, right, the sewer."

"Squeak-squeak, squeeeeeek," he replied.

"Tell me about it. Dismal conditions here. Someone ought to file a complaint with OSHA."

The rat kept squeaking, but even with my druid powers, I doubted I could have concentrated long enough to figure out what had him so upset. Maybe I was blocking the entrance to his lair? Or I'd stolen his bed. Whatever it was, he was putting up a fuss.

"Alright, alright," I mumbled, tonguing a hole in my gums where a molar used to sit. "What's the deal, little dude? Show me what you want."

"Squeak!" he replied, as if to say, "about freaking time." Then he ran through the bars of the cage and burrowed into the straw behind me.

"Whoa, little fella—what the heck are you looking for?"

I watched as he kept digging around in the straw, sticking his head out now and again to wriggle his whiskers and sniff the air. After a few minutes of this, the rat let out a loud *SQUEAK!* and sat up with something in his mouth. The rat scurried over and dropped it next to my hand, then it darted back to the other side of the bars.

"Huh, what have we here?"

I reached over with my other hand to pick it up, as the hand on that side had three dislocated fingers and a boxer's fracture. Earlier I'd punched one of the goat men in the junk, and got my hand stomped on for my trouble.

"Well, well," I said, holding up my prize. "For a rat, you are one smart cookie."

In my hand, I held a six-inch long piece of rusted baling wire. The stuff was common in these parts, since baling hay was an annual ritual for most Central Texas ranchers. I'd loaded hay bales one summer with a friend when I was in middle school and lasted all of one day. The next day I was too sore to get out of bed, and I clearly recall getting stabbed and scratched by that baling wire. Probably still had the scars.

I might have been about two head kicks away from repeating grade school, but I was still clearheaded enough to know that I could easily pick the lock on that ancient-ass cage. It took me some time to haul myself up against the bars, and I fumbled the wire more than once out of sheer exhaustion and pain, but five minutes later I was a free bird once more.

When the door swung open, I fell flat on my face and lay there for a few seconds. Then I felt something wet hit my nose. I opened my eyes, only to find the rat staring at me from close range.

"Yeah, I'm getting up. Might want to step back. I'd hate to fall and squash my rescuer."

The rat did as asked, and in my brain-addled state I didn't question it. I tried to stand by pulling myself up the bars of the cage, but after falling twice, I gave up and started crawling to the exit. Not the one that led to the sewers—hell if I was crawling through that mess again —but the one through which Butt Mandel and the goat men had left.

Butt Mandel and the Goat Men. Good name for a punk band. Heh.

Leaving a trail of blood and other bodily fluids on

the floor—don't judge, you tend to piss yourself when you take a beating that bad—I spent the next fifteen minutes crossing thirty feet of limestone floor. Once I got to the exit, I paused, listening for any sign that danger awaited on the other side. Meanwhile, the rat kept running into the next chamber and back again, squeaking like he needed my help stealing a large block of cheese. I took that to mean the coast was clear, and hauled my bloodied, battered form over the threshold and into the neighboring chamber.

As soon as I was clear of the first chamber, a sort of tingling sensation washed over me. That was my magic returning to me, and the first thing I did was shift into my full Fomorian form. Unfortunately, it really freaked the rat out, and he ran and hid somewhere in the cavern with the cage.

No wonder, I'm a monster in this form.

Roughly ten feet of twisted, deformed flesh, calloused skin, and lopsided features, I looked like a cross between Quasimodo and that big green guy from the comics, minus the emerald skin. I hated scaring the little dude, but I was dangerously close to going into shock. A full shift would require slipping out of my clothes, but it was still the fastest way to heal.

Healing did go quickly once the change was complete, and soon I was back to a functioning state. After I was healthy, hale, and whole, I shifted back into my half-Fomorian, human-looking form—no way was I squeezing out of the cave otherwise. By the time I finished getting dressed, the rat was peeking around the corner of the entrance.

"It's alright, little dude. Not going to hurt you. I just needed to change to heal."

"Squeak."

"Thanks for understanding. Any idea where they put my stuff?"

"Squeak!"

He scurried off down a side tunnel, and I followed on slightly shaky legs. Soon he led me to a natural ledge in a high-ceilinged cavern, roughly twelve feet above the floor of the cave. The rat climbed the wall like a spider, disappearing behind the ledge at the top, then reappearing dragging my Craneskin Bag by the strap in his mouth.

"That's okay—I can climb up."

Seconds later I'd retrieved my gear, and shortly after, I was strapped for battle. Granted, I was still covered in poo and blood from head to toe, but at least I was ready for a fight. Satisfied, I glanced around. Down a side tunnel, a sliver of daylight shone bright, and that was where I was headed.

"Squeak! Squeak, squeak, squeak!"

The rat was raising a fuss at my feet. I knelt down, trying to get as close to eye-to-eye—or nose to whisker —as possible.

"I take it you want to come with?"

"Squeak."

"It's gonna be dangerous. Listen, this may sound weird, but if things go sideways, just climb into my Bag. There's a lot of room in there, and it'll keep you from getting squished. Got it?"

"Squeak."

Before I knew it, the rat had climbed my leg and atop my Craneskin Bag.

"Alright, but if you have to climb inside, don't freak out, and don't touch anything. Trust me, there's some dangerous shit in there." The rat just stared at me. "Also, you need a name. How about Squeak?"

"Squeak."

"I know, not very original. I'll let you pick another name later. Right now, it's time to bust me some goat ass."

"Squa-squeeek?"

I paused, tapping a finger on my chin. "Yeah, probably best not repeat that sentence in public."

8

W ith "Squeak" safely ensconced atop my Bag, I headed toward the cave exit. Ten steps from the opening, a large shadow darkened the entrance.

Friend or foe?

I slipped into an alcove, hidden in shadow as I watched and waited. As the figure that cast the shadow came into view, all I could see was a huge, humanoid silhouette outlined by the light pouring in from outside. Whoever or whatever it was, it filled the entryway, top to bottom and side to side.

Damn, that thing is big. No horns, so not a goat man or Herr Butt Mandel. Ogre, maybe? Almost makes me wish I'd stayed in my other form. Eh, what to do?

I was still feeling somewhat weak—healing to full recovery took more than a few minutes, and I'd rushed it. It would have been preferable to sneak out and avoid a confrontation until after I had my legs back, but that thing was blocking the only exit that didn't involve slogging through a river of human filth. Acting on a snap decision, I slunk back into the cave and climbed atop the ledge where the goat men had stashed my gear.

"Squeak, you better hide," I whispered. "This could get ugly."

The rat twitched his whiskers, then he ducked inside my Craneskin Bag. *Hope he doesn't get into anything dangerous in there.* I turned my attention back to the mysterious figure, who was now cautiously creeping into the cave.

I had decent night vision in this form—not as good as a 'thrope, but decent. Still, with the backlighting from the entrance I couldn't make out much, apart from he or she was built like The Rock and wearing a hoodie. Unsure whether I should take the visitor out or wait and sneak past, I inched Dyrnwyn slightly out of its sheath.

It was a risky move, since the light might give my position away, but I'd have to draw anyway if this was going to be a fight. And, better to make life harder for me than to kill an innocent.

Hmmm, no flame. Meaning, this thing's not evil, at least not by the sword's standards. Doesn't mean it's not dangerous.

Considering my options, it occurred to me that the

cave entrance was probably hidden by an illusion. Add that fact to the size of the thing, and it was a good bet it wasn't human.

Screw it. I'll subdue it, question it, and then, if it's dangerous, I can always kill it after I get some info.

Crouching in deep shadow away from the edge, I waited silently as the massive figure crept beneath me. It moved with surprising stealth for something so large, which served as further indication I was dealing with a supernatural creature. Just as it passed the ledge, I leapt, aiming a powerful two-handed chopping blow at the base of the figure's skull. The hit wouldn't kill it, but it would probably knock it unconscious. Then, I could stick it in the cage—after removing the anti-magic glyphs from the other room and warding the bars, of course—and question it at my leisure.

Except the creature had other ideas. Whether it had heard me as I jumped or reacted out of some sort of extra-sensory perception, it spun around as I sailed through the air toward it. In one smooth motion, the giant grabbed my wrists in a huge, meaty hand, then it pivoted and tossed me effortlessly into a nearby wall.

That wall, of course, was hard limestone sediment that had formed over thousands of years, and I was flying head-first into it. I managed to twist midair, landing flat against the wall on my back with my chin tucked, narrowly avoiding another concussion. The thing was on me immediately, moving incredibly fast to grab me by the throat, slamming my back against the cavern wall as it choked me.

Instead of fighting it, I waited until it extended its arms, then I twisted, swinging my left leg over its head and the other across its chest. Latching onto its right wrist with both hands, I bridged my back and squeezed my knees together, slapping the tightest damned arm bar on it that I'd ever done.

Instead of the loud, satisfying pop of a hyperextended elbow joint, all I heard was a chuckling grunt from my opponent. You'd think that my whole body against his one arm would be an easy win, but even with near-werewolf strength, I wasn't doing a damned thing. While I was still straining to make the joint lock work, he turned and hauled his arm back as he prepared to slam my head against the wall.

Oh, hell no.

Rather than have my skull cracked open and my brains turned into scrambled eggs, I kicked off his chest as I let go of his arms. Flipping backward, I landed in a three-point stance on the floor about six feet away from the giant. This put my head right in position for a kick to the face, and sure enough, my opponent stepped forward and punted.

Gotcha.

I'd expected the attack, of course, and was ready for it. At the last second, I dodged sideways with near-vampire speed as I deflected his foot and leg to the inside. This caused him to lose his balance and land with most of his weight on his front foot. Meanwhile, I stepped behind him, boxing his ears and kicking him from behind, right between the goal posts.

The mystery giant let out a loud *oof*, then he fell to the floor clutching his family jewels. Not wanting to tangle with the thing at close range, I backed up and summoned a fireball in my hand.

Leaning forward, I held the fireball up so it illuminated the thing's face. "I swear, by my mother's bad temper, I will burn you to a crisp if you move. Now, tell me who you are and why you're here."

The thing let out a muffled moan, turning its head to face me. As it did, its hood fell back from its face, revealing very human, male features obscured by a thick, bushy red beard and mustache. Between the beard and his blue Viking eyes, I swear the guy could've been Kristofer Hivju's bigger, uglier twin.

But he was no Viking—and no ogre, either. The man dressed like a rancher, in a brown Carhartt duck canvas jacket, jeans, and lace-up steel-toed work boots. In that outfit, he could've been a local for all I knew.

Shit.

"You Colin?" he asked through gritted teeth.

"Maybe. Who's asking?"

"Does it matter?" The man had a slight German

accent, but his English was plain as day. "The Fat Man sent me, said you might need back up."

I let the fireball fizzle out a bit, maintaining a baseball-size version, just in case. "Then why'd you attack me?"

"I'd ask you the same question. Dressed as you are, covered in filth and blood and smelling like an outhouse, what was I supposed to do when you jumped out of the dark at me?"

"Eh, good point." I extinguished the fireball completely and offered a hand to help him up. He slapped it away, sitting up with a soft groan. "Sorry about kicking you in the privates."

He scowled and slowly got to his feet, leaning forward for several seconds with his hands on his knees before standing upright. "It was a good tactic. Well done. Hopefully you'll fight as well when we find the Gankerl, and their leader, Buttnmandl."

"Yeah, I already found them. They, um, escaped."

He eyed me skeptically. "You don't say."

"Ahem," I said, trying to think of a way to change the subject. About that time, Squeak popped his head out of my Craneskin Bag and climbed on top. "Hey, there you are. Thought I lost you, little dude."

"What's that?" the big man asked.

"This? This is Squeak, the rat."

"That's no rat, boy."

I shrugged. "If it looks like a rat and smells like a rat,

right? He helped me, so he comes with. Still don't know your name, though."

"Rupert. I work for the Fat Man."

I held out my hand to the big guy in the universal sign of friendship. "Nice to meet you, Rupert. No hard feelings?"

He raised an eyebrow, first looking at me, then the rat. Finally, he took my hand in a vice-like grip and shook it, once, twice, before letting go.

"No. As I said, that was well done." He glanced around the cavern, then to the door. "Any idea where they've gone?"

"Probably to crash the Christmas festivities in the town above. There's a parade tonight, and there'll easily be ten thousand people there. My bet is that they're planning something big for it."

"Meaning, we need to find them before the parade starts." He scowled even deeper. "I'd planned to ambush them here. Now, they could be anywhere."

"I thought you said you came to help me?"

Rupert *tsked*. "That was part of the plan. When I didn't find you topside, figured you'd been captured and brought to their lair."

"I wasn't captured—more like tricked." He shrugged. "Alright, so they caught me. But I escaped, all on my lonesome—" the rat squeaked loudly, interrupting me. "—with Squeak's help, that is, and I was about to go find the goat men and finish the job."

"Oh? And how are you going to do that? No telling where they're hiding now."

I reached into my pocket, pulling out a soggy tuft of goat hair. "Ever hear of a thing called sympathetic magic?"

9

As we walked out of the cave, Rupert wrinkled his nose and lengthened the distance between us considerably. "You need a bath and a change of clothes."

My olfactory nerves had apparently burned out already, as I could no longer smell a thing. "Think anyone will notice?"

"You smell like a troll. There's a reason they get their witch doctors to spell away their scent when they have to sneak around humans." He pointed to the north. "We're near the creek. Go bathe, and I'll find you some clean clothes."

I did as he suggested, freezing my lily-white tail off but feeling all the better for it afterward. My clothes were a total loss, though. Even after scrubbing them on some rocks in the creek bed, the smell persisted. I did manage to find some clean undies in my Bag, so that was a win. After slipping them on, I only had to stand a few minutes in the cold before Rupert returned.

He tossed me a plastic shopping bag. I caught it and looked inside, rummaging through the contents. The bag held a traditional German outfit of the kind men wore during Oktoberfest.

"Seriously? This was all you could find?"

Somehow, Santa's little helper had found a complete set, consisting of coverall-looking shorts made of a green velour material, a white muslin peasant shirt, some chunky-ass black dress shoes, and knee-high socks. At the bottom of the sack, I found a matching felt hat with a little white feather in the band.

"I can't wear this."

"Did you expect me to run to the megastore down the street? We have little time, so I had to grab the first thing I could find. It's a server's costume. I found it in one of the German restaurants, and it looked like your size. Look on the bright side—while wearing the lederhosen, you will blend right in with the crowd. People will think you're part of the festivities."

"People will think I showed up late for Halloween."

"Not in this town," he replied. "You can wear it, or run around naked. I do not care either way."

I exhaled heavily, then I began to get dressed. "This is so humiliating," I said after I'd put it all on. "I look like a giant Swiss leprechaun."

"There is no such thing."

"I was making a joke. Speaking of jokes, this is payback for the kick, isn't it?" Rupert's stony expression said it all. "Fine, I get it. Payback is a—"

"Watch the language," the giant man warned.

"Sheesh, you and Claus are both way too uptight. It's the new millennium, people curse in casual conversation now, you know."

"They always have," he replied, wearing the same poker face. "But just because you choose to be crass, it doesn't give you the right to subject others to your crassness."

I turned on him, a witty and slightly bawdy comeback on the tip of my tongue. But for once, I thought before speaking. "You know what? You're right. My apologies."

Rupert nodded in acknowledgement, and I figured that was as close to a "thanks" as I'd get. I finished getting dressed, pulling those stupid socks up and stuffing my feet into the shoes, which were a little tight. After donning the cap with a sigh, I turned to grab my Bag and gear, only to find Squeak sitting atop the pile looking at me.

"Squeak, squeak, squeeeek!"

"Laugh it up, fuzzball," I quoted, shooing the little guy with a gentle wave of my hand. "Keep it up, and I'll leave you in the kitty section at the local pound."

Once dressed, I stuffed everything but Dyrnwyn into

my Craneskin Bag. Nobody would think twice about me carrying a sword in this outfit. Yet, even in rural Texas, the Glock and extra magazines might raise some eyebrows at a Christmas parade.

"Are we quite done?" Rupert asked as he looked on, arms crossed over his chest. "Because we do have a town to save, and Christmas to boot. The Fat Man may have downplayed the seriousness of this crisis, as that is his way. However, I can assure you this is no joking matter."

"Can you put that in context? Claus made it sound like these jokers are just an annoyance. Yet Butt Mandel said they were going to sacrifice me to Hel later."

The large man flashed a crooked frown. "He dislikes talking about their more serious crimes against humanity. I suppose it is because his failures weigh heavily on him. I, on the other hand, will not mince words. Most of the terrorist attacks, mass shootings, murder-suicides, and the like that happen close to Christmas are incited by Krampus and his followers."

"See, this is where I get confused," I said. "I thought Krampus was a sort of Santa's helper, in a way. You know, keeping the naughty kids in line by scaring the cr —I mean, scaring the crud out of them."

Rupert chuffed at that. "And the fae are mostly benevolent creatures who grant wishes and serve as fairy godmothers to orphaned children. Come now, druid, you should know better than most that folklore has been softened over the ages. The old stories were cautionary tales, meant to warn people away from consorting with the supernatural. Now, in this age of disbelief, those stories have been altered, sugarcoated, and commercialized for mass consumption."

"Right," I replied. "And?"

"And as you also well know, the starring villains of the old legends have the greatest interest in sowing misinformation regarding their true nature."

"Makes sense to me. What are we waiting for? Give me a sec to cast this spell, then let's go kill Butt Mandel and his cankers."

"Gankerl," he said with a crooked, disapproving frown. "It means 'devil.'"

"Yeah, yeah—they all bleed the same, wet and in copious amounts," I replied as I produced the tuft of goat hair, infusing it with druid magic.

The way the spell worked, it linked the trail of scent molecules left in the air by the target's body to the tuft of hair in my hand. Then, it amplified the odor in my nostrils, increasing in intensity the closer I got. Although only useful over short distances, essentially it turned me into a bloodhound. It would be an unpleasant experience in this case, but it was the fastest way to track the goat men down.

As the spell took hold, I gagged and sneezed. "Whew, that's a powerful smell. Okay, I have a lock —let's go."

I took off at a sprint up the creek bank, emerging

from the copse of trees that had hid us from passersby. Baron's Creek ran right through old Fredericksburg, kind of parallel to Main Street, where all the festivities typically went down. The parade would run down Washington and hook a left on Main, heading all the way down to Edison and past the Marktplatz, where the town's largest Christmas display was located.

When we reached the main drag, we hit a wall of people. Folks had come out in droves, all up and down Main, enjoying the shops and restaurants while they waited for the parade to start. Working our way through the throng, I followed the scent trail west, reaching the Marktplatz in under ten minutes despite the crowd. Once we reached the plaza, we looked high and low, far and wide for signs of the goat men, but there was no sign of them in the throng.

"See anything?" I asked.

"Nothing," Rupert replied. "It's likely that Buttnmandl and the gankerl are using illusory magic to hide. In fact, they could be glamoured and standing right next to us, and we'd have no way of knowing."

"Well, I could cast a mass dispersal spell to remove any illusions in the area, but it'd wipe me out as far as magic is concerned. I'd be strictly hand-to-hand after that."

Rupert opened his mouth to answer when Squeak hopped up on my shoulder and started raising a ruckus. The giant man's brow furrowed as he stared at the rat.

Meanwhile, I plucked the rat off my shoulder, holding him in my cupped hands.

"What's up, Squeak?" The rat spun around in circles, then it stopped with its nose pointed toward the center of the plaza. "I don't understand—what do you want me to look at?"

Squeak stood up on its hind legs, raising its forelegs in the air above its head, then it did the same circle and point thing again.

"Is that creature broken?" Rupert asked.

"No, he wants us to see something." I followed the rat's nose straight ahead, to the Christmas pyramid in the center of the plaza. My eyes traveled up to the tip of the pyramid, where a weird wind vane spun slow, lazy circles. "Say, Rupert—you see anything on top of that Christmas tower?"

"It's a *Weihnachtspyramide*."

"Gesundheit."

He scowled. "It means Christmas pyramid in German."

"That's what I said. See anything up there?"

He squinted, shading his eyes even though it was almost past dusk. "*Scheiße!*"

"Hey, I thought you guys didn't cuss."

"Normally, we do not," he replied. "But this time, it is warranted. On the top level, behind the angel. See that dark figure lurking there?"

"Yeah, that's what caught my eye. Wasn't sure if it was part of the piece or not."

"It certainly is not, druid. *That* is Belsnickel."

10

"Okay, again I'm confused. I thought Belsnickel was sort of a good guy."

Rupert hissed. "There is no good in him. He once worked with the boss, fulfilling much the same role as I, but he defected to the other side centuries ago. Now he freelances for Krampus and his followers as an assassin and murderer."

"Why do I suddenly feel like I'm in a Netflix movie?" I muttered.

"What was that?"

"Nothing, nothing. So, this dude is bad news, and we have to take him out."

"Correct. Without any collateral injuries or deaths to innocents. The Fat Man doesn't like it when innocents get hurt."

"Speaking of which, why do you call him 'The Fat Man'? He looks pretty thin to me."

"That's just always been what his people call him. And he wasn't always so fit. Last year, his wife placed him on a keto diet, and although he hated it, he did lose weight. Then those images got out on social media—I'm sure you've seen them—and after Claus read the comments, he became obsessed. Whatever you do, don't ask him about it, else you'll be hearing about 'WODs' and 'Paleo eating' for hours."

"Gotcha," I said in a "sorry I asked" tone. "Back to Belsnickel—what's his kryptonite?"

"His crypto-what?"

"You know, his weakness. Vampires and 'thropes are allergic to silver, the fae hate iron, trolls can't stand sunlight, that sort of thing."

"Besides blessed objects? Mistletoe."

"Mistletoe?" I cocked my head and raised an eyebrow. "That's a bit too on the mark, don't you think?"

"You are a druid," he said as he looked down his nose at me. "Surely, you're aware that most trees and plants have medicinal or magical properties."

"Sure, rowan wood and all that. It just seems, I don't know, obvious."

"These are the descendants of Loki we're dealing with, after all. I suspect that Frigg cursed his children to make them susceptible to mistletoe, in retaliation for what happened to her favored son." Rupert looked up at the Christmas pyramid. "Belsnickel appears to be preparing something, although I can't tell what it is."

I cast a cantrip to enhance my senses and another to pierce illusions, then I focused in on the dark figure at the top of the tower. While he looked mostly human, he had a long, sharp chin, an equally long and hooked nose, upswept eyebrows, and thin lips that were pulled into a sinister sneer. He wore black fatigue pants, a black rash guard, a black watch cap, and a load-bearing vest that carried what looked to be magazines for a high-powered rifle.

"Ah sh—shoot. I think he's setting up a sniper's nest. Target-rich environment, virtually no cover, and a crowd that'll most certainly panic and stampede. If we don't stop him, this'll be a massacre."

"We could go after him, but as soon as he sees us, he'll start shooting."

"Let me think, let me think," I said as I rubbed my temple. "If I pull a gun or blast him off his perch with lightning or a fireball, it'll spook the crowd. Once they panic, we could still end up with casualties. I have some other spells I could use, but without access to the power of my Oak and Grove, casting those would wipe me out completely."

"We're running out of time, druid. Think!"

I snapped my fingers, realizing that Rupert had given me the solution. "Does that pyramid look like it's made of wood to you?"

"Some of it, yes. What do you have in mind?"

"I'm going to jack this joker up with a little druid magic. Just stay hidden and be ready to roll."

Without waiting for an answer, I pulled the stupid hat down further over my face and began snaking my way through the crowd. It was slow-going because the plaza was packed. Every so often, I'd glance up to gauge Belsnickel's progress.

Thankfully, setting up a sniper's perch wasn't as easy as it was in the movies. You didn't just snap a collapsible rifle together and go to town. You had to calculate for conditions like wind speed, humidity, temperature, and so on. Of course, with this many people, it'd be like shooting fish in a barrel, but any sniper worth their salt would be meticulous about such things.

I was almost to the pyramid when I saw a rifle barrel with a suppressor on the end poke out of the top level of the tower. Up ahead, people were waiting in a sort of queue to take selfies and photos in front of the pyramid. When I walked past the line, a large middle-aged man with a beer gut wearing a puffy vest, $300 jeans, a V-neck sweater, and a ball cap grabbed me by the arm.

"Hey, where do you think you're going? The line starts back there."

I turned to face him, resisting the urge to punch his lights out. "Sorry, sir, park maintenance. I was asked to check on the Why-Nuts-Thingie."

"The what?" the man replied.

"He means the pyramid," his much younger, blonde and buxom companion remarked distractedly as she practiced making duck faces at her phone.

"That is correct, ma'am," I said as I slipped out of her sugar daddy's grasp. "I'll be done in no time."

"Why didn't he just say so then?" I heard the man say as I vaulted the picket fence that surrounded the pyramid.

"Asshole," I muttered, sparing a nervous glance to make sure Rupert wasn't in hearing distance.

Once I was certain I wouldn't be scolded for my crass language, I laid a hand on the pyramid and closed my eyes. Dropping into a druid trance, I gathered my innate magical energies, focusing on the task at hand. This little stunt would drain me, but not completely, and it'd give Rupert the opportunity to take Belsnickel out while I located Butt Mandel and the Cankers.

Druidry was all about channeling nature's energies, but it also allowed for altering nature as well. Such magic was frowned upon, but not necessarily verboten, as we druids sometimes had to break the laws of nature for the greater good. This was one such time.

What I was attempting to do was change the physical properties of the wood in the tower, essentially transmuting it from its current state to something a bit less cozy for our friend up above. Concentrating and slowing my breathing, I extended my consciousness into the wood that made up the tower, synching with it at a molecular level. Drawing on my knowledge of the properties of wood and stone, water and air, I channeled my magic into the wood in an attempt to alter it physically and chemically.

And, I found I couldn't do it.

It's too much material—not enough juice. Shit.

Above me, my magically enhanced ears detected the distinct sound of a large caliber round being chambered in a bolt-action rifle. I had to act fast, before Belsnickel pulled that trigger. Taking a knee, I placed a hand on the earth while keeping the other on the tower.

C'mon, c'mon.

I'd never used myself as a pure conduit for the earth's energies like this, but I knew that in theory it could be done. Essentially, when I drew on the Oak and Grove's magic, I was doing the same thing. The only difference was that the Oak and Grove stored and focused those energies for me, converting them into readily available power I could tap at will.

Never before had I tried to convert pure earth energy into magic inside my body. Done wrong, I could fry myself to a crisp, short the synapses out in my brain, cause tumors to grow throughout my body, or create any number of other horrible side effects. Yet magic was nothing more than energy transmuted by thought and will—and as a druid master, theoretically nature stood at my beck and call.

Here goes nothing.

I reached down into the ground below, tuning into the phytochemical reactions occurring inside the grass between my fingers. I sensed the heat caused by microbes in the soil as they broke down waste, and the vibrations caused by thousands of people moving about all around. I also felt the wind above, blowing gently to spin the windmill blades atop the pyramid, and the water flowing and bubbling through the creek a few blocks away.

Beyond that, I sensed the negative charge of the earth, the positive charge of the atmosphere above, the heat emanating from below the earth's crust, and the thrumming tension of tectonic plates pushing against one another. For a moment, I was lost in it all, overwhelmed by the enormity of the power potentially at my command.

Must... pull back. Focus...

The fact was, I didn't need that much energy. If I went that deep, that far, not only would I burn myself out channeling it, I'd likely cause a natural disaster that would dwarf anything Belsnickel was about to do. All I really needed was enough "life force" to alter a few tons of wood, such that it would fuck up a monster's day.

So, I reached into the grass all around, and *pulled*.

11

I nstantly, my muscles strained, my veins were on fire, my nerves alight with the potential energy of half an acre of living plant life. Holding all that power was almost too much, even for just an instant. As I channeled and directed it into the wooden structure of the tower, the physical and mystical release almost caused me to pass out.

There was a flash of magic beneath my hand, then the spell transmuted all the wood in the tower from oak and pine to mistletoe instantly. Three things happened then at once. I fell to my knees, a howl of pain and agony erupted from the top of the tower, and Rupert leapt over the fence, scaling the tower like King Kong trying to save Ann Darrow from a fall.

The crazy thing was, nobody even paid attention to me, and not a soul noticed Rupert climbing the tower. A quick glance over my shoulder revealed that everyone was too busy looking at their phones or talking to friends and family to notice my little stumble. And as for Rupert, he and Belsnickel were concealed by the same sort of illusory magic that allowed the goat men to sneak around unseen.

Moments later, Santa's not-so-little helper dropped out of the tower with the would-be shooter draped over his shoulder. Belsnickel was out like a light, and covered as he was in a nasty, pustular rash, it was probably for the best.

"That's gross," I said as I pushed myself to my feet.

"*That* was impressive," Rupert said with just the tiniest hint of admiration in his voice. "I left the gun, so be sure to retrieve it later."

He made to leave, so I reached out to lay a hand on his arm. "Wait, where are you going?"

"The exposure won't keep him down forever. I need to get Belsnickel locked up before he recovers."

"What about Butt Mandel and the Cankers?"

Rupert rolled his eyes. "Must you butcher my language so? At any rate, the Fat Man chose you for a reason. After seeing that display, I am certain you can handle the Gankerl and Buttnmandl alone."

"But—"

He laid a hand on my shoulder and gave it a squeeze. "Have faith, druid. When he recruits someone for a job, the boss knows what he's about."

Before I could say anything more, he vaulted the fence and was gone. "Well, shoot. Guess it's up to me, then."

"Hey, can you get out of our shot?" It was Mr. Midlife Crisis again, mugging for the camera with his future ex-wife.

"Yeah, yeah, I'm going already," I said as I walked around the other side of the tower.

As I did, I noticed I wasn't nearly as drained as I thought. In fact, I felt pretty danged good, all things considered. It was almost as if drawing on the earth's energies had invigorated me somehow.

I wonder...

Taking a knee, I laid a hand on the earth and grass again, pulling on the same energy I'd drawn from before. I felt a tiny tingle in my hand, then it was like I'd just mainlined a pot of Luther's special nitro brew. Not only was I energized—I felt *great*.

Hopping up on the first level of the pyramid, I scanned the crowd for any sign of the goat demons. If they were around, surely I'd be able to track them by their handiwork. But everywhere I looked, things were fine. Normal, even. Everyone was laughing, smiling, and generally have a fantastic time while they waited for the parade.

"Huh."

I pulled the tuft of goat hair out, sparking the spell up again. After suffering a coughing and sneezing fit, I began to turn in a slow circle, pausing when the stench in my nostrils reached a fever pitch. Facing northeast now, horns and sirens began blaring in the distance, and people on the plaza began to fill the sidewalks along Main.

The parade—of course. They're going to ruin the parade.

While I was homing in on the goat men, the rat had crawled up on my shoulder. There he sat up, sniffing the air in the direction of Washington and Main.

"Squeak!"

"I know, little dude," I said, casting my chameleon spell on us both. "That's where I'm headed, so hang on."

Leaping over the fence and pushing people out of the way, I made like a running back as I forced a path to Main Street. Once there, I had an unimpeded line to the lead vehicles in the parade. There were fire trucks and police cars, all decked out in holiday lights and decorations, as well as convertibles carrying local celebs and community leaders, cowboys and cowgirls on prancing horses, the high school band...

...and then, the floats.

When I realized what those bleating bastards had planned, I ran at a dead sprint at the first float, dodging squad cars, baton twirlers, clowns, ponies, and people as I raced to prevent an absolutely horrible disaster.

Because there atop the first float—which happened to be a wintery scene consisting of a snowman and snowwoman skating on a frozen pond—stood the four remaining cankers, each holding a small child in their arms. The goat men were glamoured to be invisible, of course, and the children spelled asleep. Obviously, the plan was to throw the children in front of the float, where they'd be run over in full view of thousands of people.

Talk about a way to ruin Christmas.

I was roughly a block away from the float, running as fast as I could without running into anyone. Half a block ahead, I spotted something moving atop one of the buildings that lined Main Street. There, Buttnmandl danced from hoof to hoof, barely containing his excitement in anticipation of the disaster to come.

That's where they'll do it. I just have to beat them there.

Half a block from the float, I was passing the marching band when they changed formation. As they marched, they formed moving lines that weaved in and out amongst themselves, forming a very effective moving barrier of bodies that slowed me down considerably. I leapt over the first line, only to find myself caught in between two more interweaving ranks of band members.

To my right, the crowd pressed into the street, a mass of wall-to-wall people blocking my path. With no time to spare, I leapt over another group of teenagers dressed in orange and white. Landing on the other side, I faced yet another rank in my path.

I'm not going to make it.

Thinking fast, I leapt nearly vertically, landing atop an overhanging traffic light boom. Unfortunately, this placed me in direct view of both Buttnmandl and his hench-goats. The moment seemingly stretched on into infinity as I saw the goat men tense, even as they looked up at their leader above me for permission to carry out their gruesome task.

Buttnmandl opened his foul, goat-like mouth, and I knew he was about to shout his command. Acting on instinct rather than logic, I reached out to the sky with my druid senses, latching onto the static charge in the clouds high above. Using will and thought, I called down two bolts of lightning from the sky. I aimed one at the straw monstrosity standing on the roofline to my right, and the other I directed squarely at the center of the float on which the goat men stood.

The two bolts of electricity simultaneously struck with a deafening thunderclap, each hitting their intended targets. On the adjacent rooftop, Buttnmandl lit up like a torch, his brilliant, flaming form lighting up the night as he was consumed by fire. Down below, the other lightning bolt had shorted out the electrical system in the flatbed truck on which the float had been built—thankfully, without lighting the float on fire.

Tragedy averted, but we're not done yet.

As the float rolled to a stop, the goat men looked about, confused as to what they should do. Me? I drew

Dyrnwyn, holding it high above my head as I shouted a battle cry.

"Mac Cumhaill! Mac Cumhaill! Mac Cumhaill!"

On seeing me atop the traffic light boom, holding a flaming sword and screaming my head off, the goat men dropped the children atop the float and ran. I smiled and took to the rooftops, pausing to chop Buttnmandl's charred head off as I passed. Down below, folks in the crowd were rushing to help the children on the float, who were now waking up and wondering how the heck they got there.

Even after calling down that lightning, I still had some pep in my step. Even better, I now had the opportunity to pay those goat men back for kicking the crap out of me earlier. And I'd saved the people of Fredericksburg from a suffering not one, but two holiday disasters.

This was turning out to be the best Christmas ever.

12

An hour later, I was sitting in the back room of the oldest operating brewpub in Texas, sipping an Enchanted Rock Red Ale and chowing down on jager schnitzel, German potato salad, red cabbage, and hot pretzels. I was just about to get up and order another beer from the bar when someone set a pint down in front of me. I looked up to find Claus and Rupert standing on the other side of the table.

"May we sit?" the jolly man asked.

"Of course. You drinking?"

Rupert shook his head. "We never imbibe. Bad for the image."

"And the waistline," Claus added with a grin.

"It wouldn't hurt you to eat some cookies and milk every now and again," his sidekick groused. "What will the children think when they see a thin, muscular Santa

Claus pop out of their fireplace, hmm? You will scare them half to death!"

"Come now, Rupert. You know we don't do much of that work anymore."

I did a double-take, setting the pint down and leaning forward on my elbows. "You don't deliver presents on Christmas Eve anymore? Seriously?"

Claus smiled, slapping Rupert's hand as he reached for my pretzel. "Only to the poorest of households, and only under special circumstances. Mostly, we work through charities now—Blue Santa, Brown Santa, and the like."

"That's somewhat comforting," I said. "But also, oddly disappointing."

Claus chuckled softly. "Unfortunately, we live in the age of disbelief. Imagine what would happen if millions of households found extra presents under their trees? No, it wouldn't do to disturb the public peace, and according to certain authorities, the so-called 'masquerade' must be maintained."

"So now you do the hard work of keeping the bad guys in line." I pushed the remainder of my pretzel across the table to Rupert, along with a plastic condiment cup full of spicy mustard. "Who knew?"

"*Danke*," Rupert said, tucking into the bread with gusto.

Claus scowled at his assistant, but he let it slide. "With help from folks like you, of course. Speaking of which, you did a fine job here, much better than I anticipated."

"Meh, all in a day's work." I took a sip of beer, eyeing Claus over the glass. "So," I added as I set it down. "Does this mean you'll uphold your end of the bargain?"

"Of course, of course!" he replied, sounding just a tad offended. "Why would I not? Although..."

"I knew this was coming," Rupert muttered.

"Yeah?" I said, arching an eyebrow.

The jolly man's eyes dropped to the table momentarily, then his gaze swept up to meet mine. "I could use another set of hands—here, in this timeline."

"Oh? What about my 'counterpart'? Wouldn't he have something to say about that?"

Claus flashed his usual, beatific smile. "Oh, I'm sure he could be dealt with."

I pointed a finger across the table. "Smiling that way when you say something like that—you're one scary dude."

"You have no idea," Rupert interjected softly.

I pretended to think about it for several seconds, just for appearances, then I pushed myself away from the table. "I'm going to have to decline, Claus. Not that I don't appreciate the offer—coming from you, that's a real compliment. But I belong in my own timeline, and I have people counting on me there."

"I assure you," Claus said, "I can return you to your

original timeline, at the time and place of your choosing, at any juncture. Just say the word."

"You and I both know that's not the issue. After Click stranded me in the Hellpocalypse and pulled me back, for the longest time I felt like I'd abandoned Anna, Mickey, and the kids. That's why I had to go back and make it right. The same goes for the people who care about and depend on me in my primary timeline. Heck, after seeing what happens when I'm not around—again, who knew?—there's no way I'm leaving my friends and loved ones to go it alone. Nope, I gotta' go back, right to where and when Click and I were headed before you hijacked our trip to bring me here."

Claus pursed his lips. "Figured that out, did you?"

"Almost immediately. When I saw how easily you got rid of Click, I thought, 'Who else could screw up a master chronourgist's spell like that?'"

"Well—I hope you don't hold a grudge against me for it," he said with a greater than usual flush to his cheeks. "I anticipated being tied up elsewhere, and this job was a bit much for Rupert here to handle on his own, despite his many talents."

Rupert grunted at that, crossing his arms and scowling. Just then, Squeak popped his head out of my Craneskin Bag.

"Squeak?" the rat said.

Claus slapped a hand lightly on the tabletop. "Oh, and I see you found my spy!"

Squeak climbed out of the Bag and onto the table, scurrying across to Claus. He ran up the jolly old saint's arm, right into the folds of his fur-lined hood.

"The rat works for you?" I asked.

"Indeed," the jolly man replied.

"Told you it wasn't a rat," Rupert muttered. I chose to ignore his comment—some things were better left a mystery, after all.

"Well, shoot," I said with a sad shake of my head. "I'm going to miss the little guy. 'Sides, he was a big help."

"We all have our roles to play," Claus remarked. "From the smallest to the greatest. If you don't mind me saying, it was quite beneficent of you to rescue a rat, the lowliest of animals. Not to mention those children on the float."

I glanced down at my plate, scratching the stubble on my chin. "It was nothing."

"'The least of these,' dear Colin," he replied, earning a silent nod of approval from Rupert. "Now, if you're done with your meal, I believe it's time we sent you back home. Your true home, that is. Shall we?"

"The sooner the better, if you don't mind." They stood up, and I followed suit. "So, are we doing this here, in front of all these people?"

"Of course not. I prefer to avoid having to cloud the minds of those who are, shall we say, unaware of our nature." He inclined his head toward the rear exit. "Follow me, please."

Claus headed for the door, while Rupert stayed put.

"You're not coming?"

He shook his head. "Naw, got business to tidy up here before heading back to the shop."

I gave a curt nod, then I stuck out my hand. "It was a pleasure working with you, Knecht Ruprecht," I said, emphasizing the proper pronunciation.

He snort-laughed softly, taking my hand and shaking it. "And I was starting to feel bad about the lederhosen."

"Be well, Good Servant," I said, then I turned and headed after Claus.

The back door had barely closed when I reached it. I pushed it open, walking out into the cool, breezy Texas night. But as soon as I passed the threshold, I stepped into a bright, airy landscape with the noonday sun over-head. Looking around, I found myself in a field that had been plowed weeks before, facing Rube's Icehouse from across FM 1376.

I stood there a few moments waiting, just in case. Seconds later, a backpack-sized package popped into existence at my feet, wrapped in brown butcher paper and twine. A handwritten note had been tucked under the string. In ornate, looping script, it read:

Rupert said it was only fair. Merry Christmas. -C.

Upon unwrapping it, inside I discovered a complete

set of clothes in my correct size—kevlar-lined biker jeans, a downy soft black t-shirt, and an exact replica of the bullet-resistant leather jacket Maureen had given me as a gift, months before. Underneath that sat a shoebox containing a clean pair of wool socks atop of a pair of dark brown, steel-toed Doc Martens.

I was lacing up my boots when Click stumbled through a portal that appeared twenty feet away, cursing up a storm in a combination of Common Brythonic, Old Welsh, Proto-Goidelic, and English. As soon as his feet hit soil, he turned around, fists clenched at his sides and leaning forward as if to walk back through the opening, but it snapped shut in his face. I let him continue venting until I'd tied my laces, both because it amused me, and because it looked like he needed the release.

"Hey, Click," I said as I stood up, swinging Dyrnwyn's strap over my shoulder. "Good to see you."

The immortal magician and trickster spun 'round to face me, sputtering obscenities at speed until recognition sparked in his eyes. "Colin? Izzat you, lad?"

Reaching down to grab my Bag, I swung the strap over my other shoulder, taking time to adjust both sword and Bag to ensure I'd distributed the weight evenly.

"Yeah, it's me." I inclined my head toward the front entrance to Rube's Icehouse across the way. Through those doors lay the realm of The Mountain King, and no human who'd crossed them had ever returned. "I take it we're going in there?"

Click's brow furrowed, and for several long moments he stared at me like a calf at a new gate. He blinked and rubbed his eyes, then he turned his gaze toward Rube's, and finally at me again. Just like that, his expression softened and he smiled broadly.

"Right ya' are, lad. Ready ta' go rescue that flame-haired lass from certain death?"

I chuckled softly. "Sure, Click. Lead the way."

As Click walked off toward the tavern, I paused and took in a long, deep breath of fresh Texas air.

It's good to be home.

This concludes *Colin McCool Saves Christmas*. Never fear, Colin's adventures *will* continue in *Druid's Bane*, the third installment in The Trickster Cycle series of Druidverse novels!

Visit my website at MDMassey.com and subscribe to download two FREE books today. When you do, you'll be added to my notification list, so you can be among the first to hear about new releases, sales, book signing events, and more.

ABOUT THE AUTHOR

M.D. Massey describes himself as the prototypical INTJ. He's been a combat medic, an emergency room technician, a fitness trainer, a truck driver, a martial arts instructor, a cook, a business consultant, a web designer, and a security professional.

If there's one thing readers say about his novels, it's that Massey makes the fantastic seem real. His eclectic background provides him with a rich tapestry of experiences to draw on when crafting fiction, as evidenced by the believable worlds and relatable characters he creates.

Mr. Massey lives in Austin, Texas with his family and a huge American Bulldog that keeps him company while he writes. When he's not in his office or at the local coffee shop writing, you can find him in his garage pummeling inanimate objects, or knife fighting with his friends.

 facebook.com/mdmasseyauthor